Two Cavapoo

A Cavapoo Family

by Jessica Pryce   Illustrated by TullipStudio

For dog lovers everywhere

For:

From:

For permission requests, write to the publisher, addressed "Attention:
Permissions Coordinator," 205 N. Michigan Avenue, Suite #810, Chicago,
IL 60601. 13th & Joan books may be purchased for educational,
business or sales promotional use. For information, please email the Sales
Department at sales@13thandjoan.com.

Printed in the U. S. A. First Printing,
Library of Congress Cataloging-in-Publication Data has been applied for.
ISBN: 978-1-7326464-7-6

Chapter 1

Carson was so excited that she could hardly sleep.

Tomorrow, she'll be getting a new puppy for her 10th birthday!

Rocky and Apollo are cavapoo puppies.
They are brothers and best friends. Their
mother's name is Miracle. Their father's
name is Charles.

There were 6 puppies, and most have
been adopted. But, Rocky and Apollo still
needed a family.

All of the dogs lived with Carson's Auntie Leesha.

There were two left and Carson will get to choose one to take home.

The next morning, Carson ran to brush her teeth so fast that her mommy erupted into laughter. "Oh, Carson! I've never seen you move so fast to brush your teeth. I like your new puppy already!"

Carson's father (whose name is also Carson) came out of his room and joined them.
"You must be excited, Lil C!" he laughed, calling Carson by her nickname.

"Understatement!" Carson hugged him.
"How long is the drive to Auntie's house?"

"About two hours," he answered.
"I can't wait!" Carson announced.

08

"Can I name my new puppy?" Carson asked when she got into the car.

"I think that's a great idea, Lil C!" Daddy said. "How about we name him 'Carson?'"

"I think we have enough Carsons in the house," Mommy replied.

"Fair enough!" Daddy said. They all laughed.

Chapter 2

When Carson and her parents arrived, the two cavapoo were napping with their mom, Miracle.

"Hi, Auntie!" Carson ran into her Aunt's arms for a hug.

"Hi, Lil C!" Auntie squeezed her tightly. The puppies stirred awake when they heard the visitors.

Carson and her aunt walked over to the puppies. "They are so adorable!" Carson squealed, in a whisper, so she did not frighten the puppies.

"I call him Rocky," her aunt pointed. "And that's Apollo. But, it's not too late to rename the one you pick."

Rocky was a bright tan color with a singular strip of white that started on top of his head and went down his face and neck. Apollo was a copper brown. When Carson lifted up Rocky, Apollo tried to jump into her arms to join his brother.

"They really love each other," her aunt laughed. "They don't like to be apart."

Carson picked up Apollo in her other arm, and both puppies touched their noses together.

"So, which puppy do you want to take home?" Daddy asked as he joined Carson on the floor. "It will be hard to pick."

Carson looked at her dad, then down at both puppies, and smiled. She had an idea.

"Now, hear me out," Carson began.

Both of her parents looked at each other and laughed.

Carson promised her parents that she would take good care of the puppies if they let her take them both.

"Two puppies can be a handful, Lil C,"
her parents warned.

"I know!" Carson held up both puppies and giggled.
Carson's parents were quiet and thinking.
Could they handle two puppies?

18

Chapter 3

Carson's parents said yes!

"Yippee! I'm your new mom," Carson said to the puppies.

"Or am I their big sister?" she asked her parents.

"Well, I'm a bit too young to be a grandpa," Daddy said.

Mommy laughed. "That makes two of us. Lil C, looks like you're a big sister."

"I like it! Besides, Rocky and Apollo don't need a mother. They have Miracle."

Carson's parents began to pack up the car to leave. "What about their names?" Auntie asked Carson.

Carson gave both puppies a quick kiss on the top of their heads.

"I think I want to keep calling them Rocky and Apollo. Is that okay?"

"Of course. I think it fits them nicely." Auntie hugged both puppies.

"Enjoy your new family, boys."

Carson got settled into the car with her two cavapoo.

"Mommy, how long before we're home?"

"About two hours, Lil C."

"I can't wait."

Next in the Series:

Two Cavapoo: A Cavapoo Day at School

Jessica Pryce was born and raised in Polk County, Florida. She loves writing, playing tennis and collecting books. She has been an avid reader for as long as she can remember. She refers to reading as a superpower... not a hobby.

She's thrilled to create opportunities for children to read. She is a fairly new dog-mom and she is enjoying the adventure. Jessica still resides in Florida with her two cavapoo, Rocky and Apollo.

You can stay up to date on new book releases by following on Instagram: @twocavapoobook

You can also stay connected to Jessica on Instagram: @writersgottaread

Printed in the USA
CPSIA information can be obtained
at www.ICGtesting.com
LVHW061514261123
764962LV00011B/203